H.G. Wells' impressive literary achievements were extremely diverse, yet he was always best known for his "scientific romances." **The Island of Dr. Moreau** (1896) was the third in Wells' long line of scientific romances, preceded by *The Time Machine* and *The Wonderful Visit* (1895), and followed by such works as *The Invisible Man* (1897), *The War of the Worlds* (1898), and *The First Men in the Moon* (1901). With these novels, Wells defined a popular new literary genre that is now known as science fiction. Wells' fantasies were always distinguished by their critical, as well as popular, success. While readers delighted in the imaginative stories, critics and scholars were intrigued by Wells' blend of satire, warnings about the possible dangers of new scientific advancements, and predictions of new social orders. Wells' preoccupation with both social and scientific progress stemmed from his part in the nineteenth century's great scientific/religious debates, in which the ethics and morals of the two estates were argued and questioned. Wells took a middle ground in that philosophical struggle. He believed in the potential of science to help create a utopia, but, at the same time, he recognized the disaster that could result from the misuse of knowledge. He believed in social order, but felt that humanity had to be ready to shed old systems in order to achieve a higher standard of existence. That conflict is what makes **The Island of Dr. Moreau** so compelling, so frightening — "an atrocious miracle," as Jorge Luis Borges has called it. Science's promise of a better life is shattered when Moreau, a man of uncompromising logic, abuses his knowledge. At the same time, the island's social order unravels when its unreasoning creatures cannot recognize that their cultural structure is the source of their misery. To survive, Wells argued, we must carefully consider the potential effects of any action *or* inaction. As dark as his vision is in **The Island of Dr. Moreau**, there remains a light, a caution — a lesson.

The Island of Dr. Moreau
Classics Illustrated, Number 12

Wade Roberts, Editorial Director
Alex Wald, Art Director
Mike McCormick, Production Manager

PRINTING HISTORY
1st edition published August 1990

Copyright © 1990 by The Berkley Publishing Group and First Publishing, Inc. All rights reserved. No part of this book may be reproduced or transmitted in any form or by any means, electronic or mechanical, including photocopying, recording, or by information storage and retrieval system, without express written permission from the publishers.

For information, address: First Publishing, Inc., 435 North LaSalle St., Chicago, Illinois 60610.

ISBN 0-425-12029-5

TRADEMARK NOTICE: Classics Illustrated® is a registered trademark of Frawley Corporation. The Classics Illustrated logo is a trademark of The Berkley Publishing Group and First Publishing, Inc. "Berkley" and the stylized "B" are trademarks of The Berkley Publishing Group. "First Publishing" and the stylized "1F" are trademarks belonging to First Publishing, Inc.

Distributed by Berkley Sales & Marketing, a division of The Berkley Publishing Group, 200 Madison Avenue, New York, New York 10016.

Printed in the United States of America
1 2 3 4 5 6 7 8 9 0

THE MOREAU HORRORS. THAT LONG-FORGOTTEN PAMPHLET CAME BACK WITH STARTLING VIVIDNESS TO MY MIND.

I HAD BEEN A MERE LAD THEN, AND MOREAU WAS, I SUPPOSE, ABOUT FIFTY.

A PROMINENT AND MASTERFUL PHYSIOLOGIST, WELL KNOWN IN SCIENTIFIC CIRCLES FOR HIS EXTRAORDINARY IMAGINATION.

RATTLE...

SUDDENLY HIS CAREER HAD CLOSED. HE HAD TO LEAVE ENGLAND. A JOURNALIST OBTAINED ACCESS TO HIS LABORATORY.

I HEARD THE PUMA GROWLING THROUGH THE WALL, AND ONE OF THE DOGS YELPED AS IF IT HAD BEEN STRUCK.

YOUR BREAKFAST, SAIR.

AN ODOR THAT HAD BEEN IN THE BACKGROUND OF MY THOUGHTS SUDDENLY CAME FORWARD.

IT WAS THE ANTISEPTIC ODOR OF THE OPERATING ROOM.

WITH THE HELP OF A SHOCKING ACCIDENT-- IF IT WAS AN ACCIDENT-- HIS GRUESOME PAMPHLET BECAME NOTORIOUS.

ON THE DAY OF ITS PUBLICATION, A WRETCHED DOG, FLAYED AND OTHERWISE MUTILATED, ESCAPED FROM MOREAU'S HOUSE.

WHAT COULD IT MEAN? A LOCKED ENCLOSURE, A NOTORIOUS VIVISECTOR, AND THESE CRIPPLED AND DISTORTED MEN?...

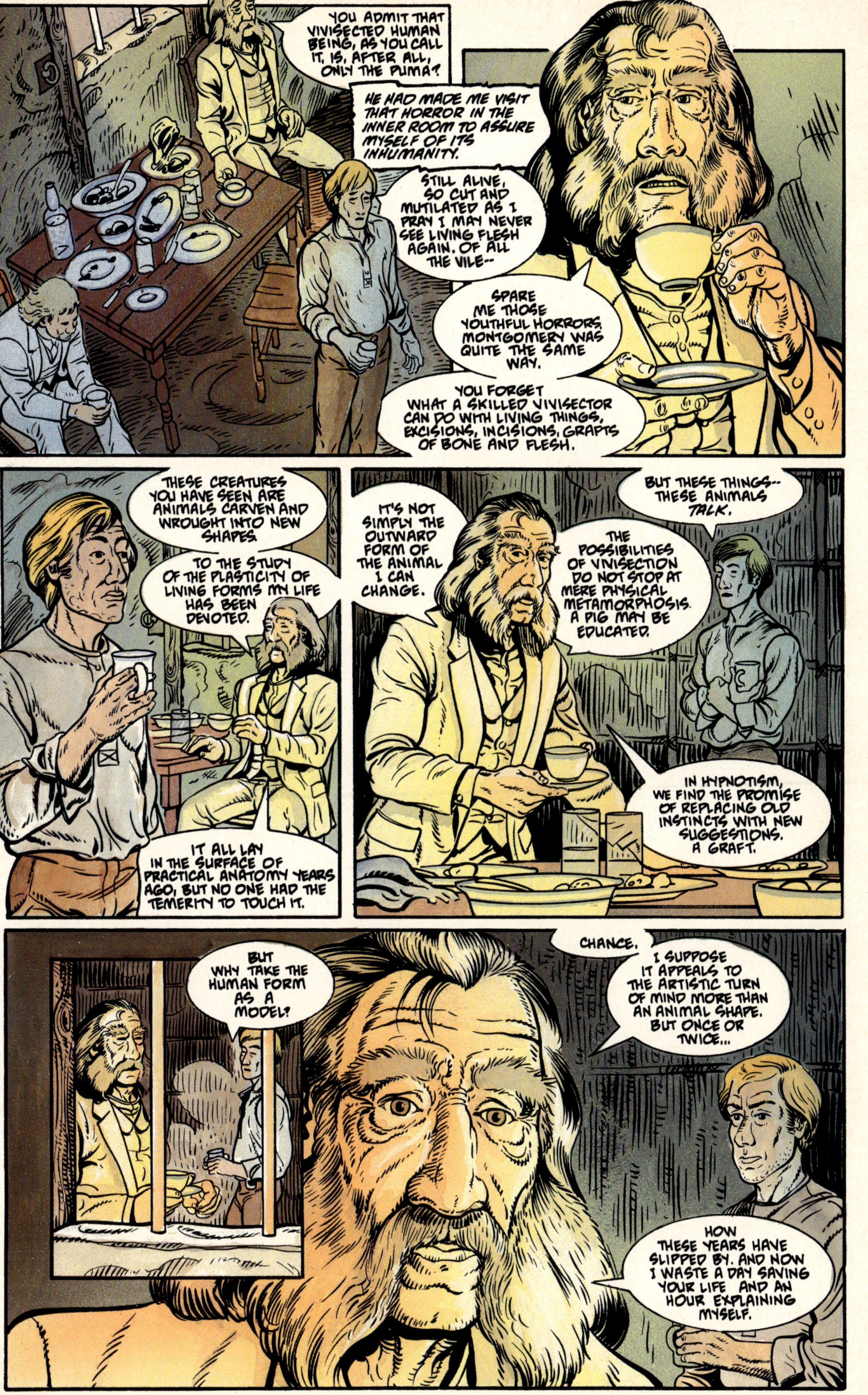

I KNEW AT ONCE WHAT HAD HAPPENED.

WHEN I HAD RUSHED TO MONTGOMERY'S ASSISTANCE, I HAD OVERTURNED THE LAMP.

THE ENCLOSURE, WITH ALL ITS PROVISIONS, BURNT NOISILY, WITH SUDDEN GUSTS OF FLAME.

BEFORE ME WAS THE GLITTERING DESOLATION OF THE SEA; BEHIND ME, THE ISLAND, ITS BEAST PEOPLE SILENT AND UNSEEN.

ON THE THIRD DAY, I WAS PICKED UP BY A BRIG FROM APIA TO SAN FRANCISCO.

IT IS STRANGE, BUT I FELT NO DESIRE TO RETURN TO MANKIND. I WAS ONLY GLAD TO BE QUIT OF THE FOULNESS OF THE BEAST MONSTERS.

NEITHER THE CAPTAIN OR MATE WOULD BELIEVE MY STORY. I REFRAINED FROM TELLING MY ADVENTURE FURTHER.

THEY SAY THAT TERROR IS A DISEASE, AND I CAN WITNESS THAT A RESTLESS FEAR HAS DWELT IN MY MIND.

I LOOK ABOUT ME AT MY FELLOW MEN, AND I GO IN FEAR.

I FEEL AS THOUGH THE ANIMAL IS SURGING UP THROUGH THEM, THAT PRESENTLY THE DEGRADATION OF THE ISLANDERS WILL BE PLAYED OVER AGAIN ON A LARGER SCALE.

I KNOW THIS IS AN ILLUSION, YET I SHRINK FROM THEM AND LONG TO BE AWAY FROM THEM AND ALONE.

BUT THIS IS A MOOD THAT COMES TO ME NOW RARELY. THERE IS, I DO NOT KNOW HOW OR WHY, A SENSE OF INFINITE PEACE AND PROTECTION IN THE GLITTERING HOSTS OF HEAVEN.

THERE IT MUST BE, I THINK, IN THE VAST AND ETERNAL LAWS OF MATTER, NOT IN THE DAILY CARES AND SINS AND TROUBLES OF MEN.

I HOPE, OR I COULD NOT LIVE. AND SO, IN HOPE AND SOLITUDE, MY STORY ENDS.

Edward Prendick

H.G. WELLS was born in Bromley, Kent, England, on September 21, 1866, the son of an unsuccessful small businessman and a domestic servant. In 1884, Wells won a scholarship to the University of London, where he was strongly influenced by Thomas Huxley, the famed Darwinian biologist. Wells' early novel, *The Time Machine* (1895), reflected his lifelong fascination with science. Described as a "scientific romance," *The Time Machine* was a popular success, and contributed greatly to the critical acceptance of literature that blended fiction with scientific theory and predictions. Although he was preceded by the French fantasist Jules Verne, Wells — whose works combined conjecture, adventure, satire, and social and political theories — was considered the first great serious writer of what came to be known as science fiction. In quick succession, he wrote *The Island of Dr. Moreau* (1896), *The Invisible Man* (1897), *The War of the Worlds* (1899), and *The First Men in the Moon* (1901). In 1903, Wells joined England's socialist Fabian Society; impatient and independent, he soon left after a disagreement with his sponsor, the playwright George Bernard Shaw. After the turn of the century, Wells produced a number of widely read novels that mirrored his interest in feminism, socialism and nationalism. Those works, such as *Tono-Bungay* (1909), and *The New Machiavelli* (1911), earned Wells a role as an influential social commentator. Although twice-wed, Wells was an outspoken critic of conventional marriage; his one child, a son, was born out of wedlock in 1914 to the novelist Rebecca West. With the publication of the massive *The Outline of History* (1920), and its briefer offspring, *A Short History of the World* (1922), Wells' following continued to grow. Throughout his life, Wells was greatly concerned about the survival of society, and depicted his dreams of an ideal world in books like *Men Like Gods* (1923), and *The Shape of Things to Come* (1933); some of his visions included world government by supermen, and a new religion based on physics. His later years, though, were marked by fear that technological advances were outdistancing intellectual, moral, and social development. *Mind at the End of Its Tether* (1945), Wells' last work, was a despairing prediction of humanity's future. Wells died in 1946, not long after the first use of atomic weapons.

ERIC VINCENT was born in Gainesville, Florida, in 1953, and graduated from the University of Southwestern Louisiana. Vincent has spent 15 years in advertising, as an art director, illustrator, writer, director and producer. He has published his own magazine, *Cerberus*, and has worked as a newspaper illustrator and cartoonist. Vincent has illustrated four children's books. One of those, *Clovis Crawfish and the Orphan Zo-Zo*, won the 1984 Children's Choice Award; another, *Henry Hamilton, Graduate Ghost*, was adapted into a television special. Vincent's comics credits include the critically acclaimed *Alien Fire*.

STEVEN GRANT was born in Madison, Wisconsin, in 1953, and graduated from the University of Wisconsin. Grant's comics credits include *Twilight Man, Whisper, Punisher,* and *Life of Pope John Paul II.* The former editor-in-chief of the *Velvet Light Trap Review of Cinema,* Grant has written music criticism for *Trouser Press,* and has contributed to several books on popular culture, including *Close-Ups* and *The Rock Yearbook.* Grant also has written a variety of widely praised young-adult adventure novels.

"The BEST OZ BOOKS since L. Frank Baum"

— **Don Thompson**, *Comics Buyer's Guide*

From the publishers of **CLASSICS ILLUSTRATED** comes an all-new series of original Oz adventures founded on and continuing the famous OZ stories of L. Frank Baum.

Written and illustrated by master storyteller **Eric Shanower**, each perfect bound 48 page volume is lavishly illustrated in full color and measures a large 8"x11."

Please send me the following all-new Oz books by Eric Shanower. I have checked my selections below and have added $2.00 per title U.S. ($3.00 per title Canadian) for postage and handling (Illinois residents must add 8% sales tax). I have enclosed my check or money order in U.S. funds for $ _____ .

Title	U.S.	CANADA
___ The Enchanted Apples of Oz.	$7.95	$10.95
___ The Secret Island of Oz.	$7.95	$10.95
___ The Ice King of Oz.	$7.95	$10.95
___ The Forgotten Forest of Oz.	$8.95	$10.95

Sorry, no foreign orders. Please make checks payable to First Publishing, Inc. Please allow 6-8 weeks for delivery.

Name _____ Address _____
City _____ State _____ Zip _____

Mail to: OZ, Dept. DM, First Publishing, Inc. 435 North LaSalle Street Chicago, IL 606
Offer Expires October 31, 1990